Baba Yaga

Written by Tony Bradman

Illustrated by Anaïs Goldemberg

to Alcsoja

D1638082

OXFORD

UNIVERSITY PRESS

Once upon a time, there was a little Russian girl called Natasha. Her mother had died when she was a baby, but she and her father were very happy. Until he got married again, that is…

Natasha was sweet, kind and clever. Yet her father's new wife hated her and was horrible when he wasn't around.

One day her stepmother told Natasha she had a special job for her to do.

"I, um… need to borrow a needle and thread from my sister," said the stepmother, with a wicked grin. "Off you go now. She lives deep in the forest, and her name is… Baba Yaga."

Natasha's heart sank. She knew her stepmother was up to something. Natasha didn't like the sound of this sister. She had heard some people say that Baba Yaga was an evil witch.

Natasha tried hard to get out of it, but her stepmother said she had to go. So Natasha sighed, tied up some scraps of food in an old napkin to keep her going, and headed  towards the dark wood.

"I have a bad feeling about this..." she muttered
as she walked along.

She walked across the fields and into the forest,
and came at last to a clearing. There she saw the
strangest sight. A hut standing on giant chicken legs!

Natasha opened the gate, and it squeaked almost as if it was in pain.

"Why, you poor old thing!" she said, and gave it some oil from a can she found nearby.

Next, a big, scary dog growled at her. She calmed him down with some food from her napkin and some kind words.

Then Baba Yaga herself appeared...

She had burning red eyes, and teeth made of iron. Natasha gulped.

"Please, Baba Yaga," she said. "Your sister wants to borrow a needle and thread."

"Is that so?" said the witch. She licked her thin lips and looked Natasha up and down. "Well, you'd better come and wait in my hut while I find them, my dear."

Baba Yaga whistled
and the hut came
running over. Natasha
climbed up nervously
and stood in the gloom.
The only light came from
a big iron stove in the
corner.

"Make yourself at home," said Baba Yaga with
a wicked smile. "I'll be back in a moment. It's
getting late, perhaps you'd like to stay for dinner?"

The witch didn't wait for an answer and hurried off. Natasha peeped out. She saw Baba Yaga wasn't looking for a needle and thread at all, she was fetching wood for the stove.

"You do realise you're the only item on the menu, don't you?" hissed a soft voice behind Natasha. "Baba Yaga just loves to eat sweet little girls."

Natasha turned around.
A terribly thin black cat came
out of the shadows.

"Well, I knew she wasn't very
nice," said Natasha with a frown.
"And I can see she doesn't feed
you much, either. Here, have my
last few scraps of food."

"What a kind girl you are!"
said the cat, surprised. "You
know, I might be able to help
you …"

"Take these … and run for your life," said the cat.
He gave her

a towel,

a comb

and a small stone.

"Throw each one behind you when Baba Yaga gets close."

Natasha thanked the cat and quietly jumped down from the hut. The dog saw her go but didn't bark, and the gate opened and closed without a squeak.

The witch was very
cross indeed when she
found out her dinner had
run off.

"You should have warned
me!" she yelled at the cat, the
dog and the gate.

"Why?" said the cat.
"She was nice to us and
you've always been horrid!"

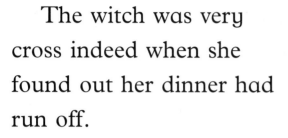

Baba Yaga scowled and stamped her foot.
Then she hurried off after Natasha.

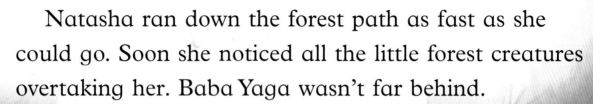

Natasha ran down the forest path as fast as she could go. Soon she noticed all the little forest creatures overtaking her. Baba Yaga wasn't far behind.

"You might as well give up now!" yelled the witch.
"You won't get away!"

Natasha kept running, but Baba Yaga was on the point of catching her ...

Suddenly, Natasha remembered the things she was carrying and the wise words of the cat. She threw the towel behind her and it turned into a raging river between her and the witch.

"Bother!" shouted Baba Yaga,
shaking her fist.

"Phew!" thought Natasha. But
Baba Yaga simply drank the river,
and Natasha ran off once more.

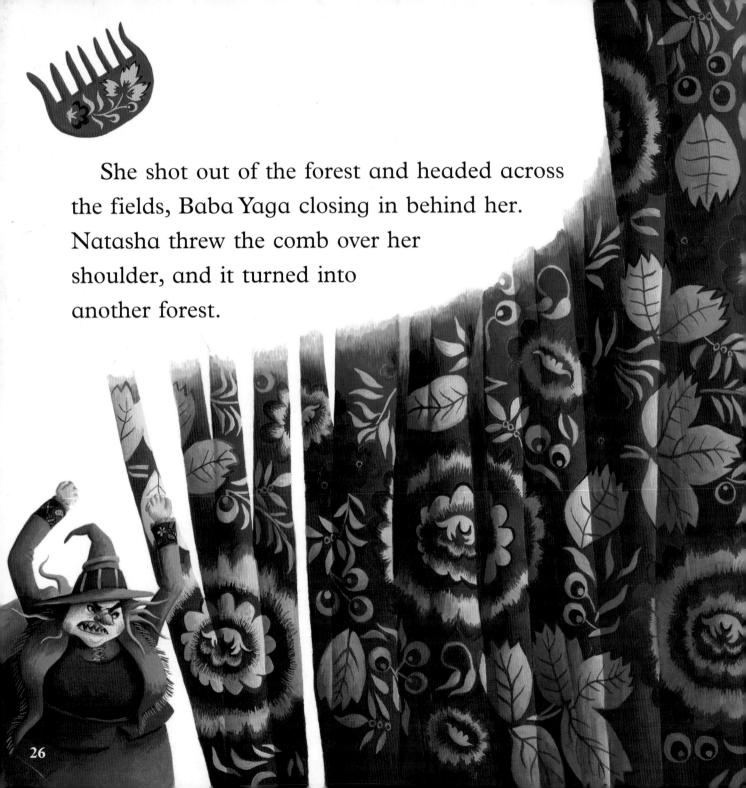

She shot out of the forest and headed across
the fields, Baba Yaga closing in behind her.
Natasha threw the comb over her
shoulder, and it turned into
another forest.

"BOTHER!" screamed Baba Yaga, shaking her fists. Before Natasha could even think "Phew!", the witch started chewing a path through the trees.

27

Baba Yaga kept on coming, and
Natasha knew she only had one chance
left. The witch was almost on top of her
when she threw the small stone.

And this time Baba Yaga was beaten.
The stone turned into ... a mountain!
"Serves you right!" said Natasha
with a smile. Then she headed for home.

Her stepmother was very surprised to see her. Natasha told her father all about what had happened and how her stepmother had planned it all along. He was so cross, he told his wife to pack her bags and get out of their lives forever.

"Good riddance to bad rubbish!" he
said. Natasha smiled. She had to agree.

Once upon a time...

The end.